All Th
Folktales & Rhymes

Kelden

Acknowledgments

I am nothing without my family, who have supported me and my wild, and often wicked, storytelling so thoroughly throughout the years. So, as always, thank you Mom, Dad, Breanna, Colton, and Alexis.

If I'm nothing without my family, I'd truly be lost without my friends. Thank you for listening and reading my work, providing helpful feedback, and proofing. Special thanks to Veles, Thorn, Meegan, Lilith, Matthew, Markus, and Jackson.

And of course, thank you to Little Tom Browncoat. I love you to the Moon and to Saturn.

To my brother, with whom my imagination grew.

Table of Contents

Introduction

A brilliant fire burns in a circle of stones upon the ground,
casting shadows in the woods surrounding us. We've been
enjoying our time out in the wild, with the full moon hanging
high above the trees. But the conversation has faded and for a
while, we've simply listened to the crackling of the bonfire and
the occasional hooting of an owl. But the hour has gotten late
and there is a noticeable shift in the atmosphere, an unease
creeping in upon us from the darkness. Suddenly, a coyote
howls from somewhere off in the distance. You whip your
head in the direction of the eerie call and when you turn back,
I notice the look of trepidation on your face.

I lean in close from across the fire and whisper, "Do you
want to hear a story?"

••••

Storytelling is a powerful magic, one that has always been
a passion of mine. The process of weaving together details
to form a moving narrative is nothing short of alchemical.
There are many types of stories, but those which I love
most, and that which you'll find in this volume, are
folktales and rhymes. My life and my practice as a Witch,
as I'm sure is true for many readers, are informed by
folklore. Whether it's the fashioning of apotropaic
charms, a journey to the nocturnal Sabbath, or belief in a
myriad of eldritch beings. The folktales and rhymes
within these pages are a mixture of original and
re-imagined pieces, each infused with such classical lore.

1

Please refer to the Notes section at the back of the book for further information on source material when applicable.

While my hope is that these folktales and rhymes provide you, and those with whom you share them, with entertainment and chills, remember that there is often more to the story than what appears upon first reading or listening. Keep your eyes and ears open, for the curious mind can pick up on the valuable lessons just below the surface. In this case, you just might gather insights into the art of Witchery in its many facets and forms.

So, with that said, stoke the fire, grab your drink of choice, and prepare to enter the magical and spooky world of all them Witches.

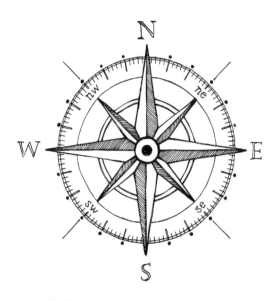

The Compass Quest

Tettens, Tettens, great ruler of North,
Here I do come, please let me now forth.
Into your realm of wind and of air,
Of tempest gales and breezes fair.
May my spirit learn of wisdom great,
As I travel through your blackest gate.

Lucet, Lucet, to you I now go,
Great ruler of East, the way please show.
Into your realm of heat and of fire,
Of ember's spark and inferno pyre.
May my spirit burn with passion more,
As I enter through your crimson door.

Carenos, Carenos, to you I turn,
Great ruler of South, for entry I yearn.
Into your realm of earth and of stone,
Of twisted roots and old buried bone.
May my spirit's strength grow ever keen,
As I walk along your trail of green.

Noden, Noden, great ruler of West,
Here I do come, to finish my quest.
In your realm of water and of sea,
Of thundering falls and rivers free.
May my spirit now be healed by you,
As I move across your bridge so blue.

The Greedy-Hearted Witch

There was once a spirit who lived within a grove of looming, ancient pines. And this spirit cared deeply for a young Witch who would come to visit nearly every day. The Witch would talk with the spirit, who had sadly gone unnoticed for so long. The Witch would speak kind words and sing to the spirit. The Witch would offer small cakes and, in exchange, the spirit would grant him small favors. Together they worked wondrous magic.

And so, the spirit was happy.

But as time went on, the Witch grew older and his visits to the grove of pines became fewer. This saddened the spirit, who started to miss their dear friend.

Then one day the Witch returned and, in their excitement, the spirit called out, "Come Witch, sing to me, feed me small cakes, ask of me your favors, and we will work magic together."

"I am too busy to sing and have no small cakes to give," replied the Witch. "I want success. I want money. Can you give me what I ask?"

"I'm sorry," said the spirit, "but I have no money to give. I have only the virtues of prosperity. Take some of my magic. Then you will have what you've asked for and you will be happy."

So, the Witch took the virtues of prosperity from the spirit and left. At first, the spirit was overjoyed about having seen their old friend and having offered him a helping hand.

But again, the Witch stayed away for a long while and the spirit felt sad once more.

Then one day the Witch returned. The spirit shook with delight and called out, "Come Witch, feed me small cakes, ask of me your favors, and we will work magic together."

"I have no small cakes to give," replied the Witch. "I want romance. I want a wife. Can you give me what I ask?"

"I'm sorry," said the spirit, "but I have no wife to give. I have only the virtues of love. Take some of my magic. Then you will have what you've asked for and you will be happy."

So, the Witch took the virtues of love from the spirit and left. At first, the spirit felt pleased, for yet again they had been able to help their old friend.

But just as before, the Witch stayed away for a long while and the spirit came to feel disappointed.

Then one day the Witch returned. The spirit was so elated that their voice trembled as they called out, "Come Witch, come and work magic."

"I have no time to work magic," replied the Witch. "I want status. I want authority. Can you give me what I ask?"

"I'm sorry," said the spirit, "but I have no authority to give. I have only the virtues of sovereignty. Take some of my magic. Then you will have what you've asked for and you will be happy."

So, the Witch took the virtues of sovereignty from the spirit and left. But unlike before, the spirit was now unsure of how they felt regarding their old friend.

And after a long period had passed the Witch returned. This time though, the spirit spoke not with excitement, nor delight, nor elation when they said, "I am sorry Witch, but I have nothing left to give you. You've taken my virtues of sovereignty. You cannot have anymore."

"I have authority over many, I have no use for your virtues of sovereignty," replied the Witch.

"You've taken my virtues of love," said the spirit. "You cannot have anymore."

"I have an obedient wife, I have no use for your virtues of love," replied the Witch.

"You've taken my virtues of prosperity," said the spirit. "You cannot have anymore."

"I have all the money I need, I have no use for your virtues of prosperity," replied the Witch. "I am an old man now and my health is failing. It is your virtues of healing that I need, so that I may get better and continue living my life."

"I'm sorry," said the spirit. "But you have taken and taken from me and given nothing in return. You have disrespected me and I can no longer help you."

"But you're my spirit," the Witch protested incredulously.

"Do not be so mistaken my old friend, I belong to no one," declared the spirit. "You have abused my kindness and now you must go. Leave me be and do not come back."

So, the Witch left, never to return to the grove of pines again.

And although it took some time, the spirit eventually grew to be happy once more.

The Goat Song

Black goat, gray goat, where is it you go?
To the merry Sabbath, if really you must know.

Black goat, gray goat, can I come along?
Yes child, yes child, do join my eldritch throng.

Black goat, gray goat, who will all be there?
Witches and ghosts and the Folk who are most Fair.

Black goat, gray goat, what will we have to sup?
Blackest bread and darkest wine served in a horse hoof
cup.

Black goat, gray goat, what will we do for fun?
Around the fire, we shall dance, a ring against the sun.

Black goat, gray goat, will there be work to do?
But of course, mischievous work and wicked deeds too.

Black goat, gray goat, may I be the Queen?
Yes child, yes child, in the world unseen.

The Halloween Hunt

There was once a young boy who lived in a quaint little town on the edge of a deep, dark stretch of woods. The boy, who had a timid heart, was often the victim of cruel pranks played on him by the other children in town. These vicious children especially enjoyed subjecting the young boy to ghastly tales which turned his face white and his legs to jelly. Oh, how the other children laughed at the young boy who was so easily spooked. But as it was fated, one Halloween night everything changed....

It was a particularly windy night and nearly all the creaky old trees were devoid of their leaves. Their skeletal branches swayed violently against the purple-gray sky. Outside his house, the young boy found himself surrounded by those nasty children who once again teased him without mercy.

"It's Halloween night," said the first child, "You know what that means, scaredy mouse!"

"The Black Woodsman is on the prowl, looking for his prey!" jeered the second.

"He always comes to take the weak and fearful." Cackled the third. "Just like you little mouse!"

The young boy knew the legend well, for it had been whispered for centuries, as long as anyone in town could remember. On Halloween night, the Black Woodsman rode through the forest with his hellhounds, collecting the souls of those unfortunate enough to cross his path. It was said that if you were to hear the winding of his horn, it was a sure sign that you were next. The Woodsman would ride up on his giant black horse and scoop you up before you could even blink. He'd drag you away, your screams trailing behind on the wind. Come morning, the only thing left of you to find would be your shoes, which had turned into nothing more than a smoking pile of ash.

"I am not afraid!" The young boy declared in defiance, though his body shook.

"He'll get you good tonight pitiful mouse!" Laughed the first child.

"He'll take you into the deep, dark woods, straight on down to hell!" Added the second

"Shh! Quiet, what's that sound?" Hushed the third.

The wind was howling through the trees, but beyond it the young boy could hear something else. His blood ran cold as he recognized the haunting echo of a hunting horn. Instantly, his facade of bravery shattered and he was unable to stop himself from crying out in fear.

"He's coming to get you!" The other children chanted over and over, dancing around the young boy.

The horn blew louder and louder, getting closer and closer. The young boy fell to the ground, covering his ears with his hands and squeezing his eyes shut tight. Yet just as he thought that Black Woodsman was upon him, the noise stopped. The other children erupted into a fit of laughter, nearly bursting at the seams. The young boy slowly opened his eyes, only to see a fourth child emerge carrying a horn.

"What a terrified little mouse!" Said the fourth child.

"What a pathetic little mouse!" Said the others.

The young boy got to his feet, wiping tears from his eyes. He turned on his heel and ran into his house, slamming the door on the sound of the children's ruthless taunts.

Later that night, the young boy sat on his bed. The fear he had felt earlier had been replaced with an anger that burnt within his heart. He was tired of being scared and he was most certainly tired of being bullied. The more he thought about the other children the more he felt enraged. He walked to his window and threw it open, allowing the wild night wind to whip against his face. He clung to the windowsill, the fury inside him so red-hot that his fingers left scorch marks upon the wood.

"I wish the Black Woodsman would come," The young boy said aloud. "For I am *not* afraid."

And so, as often is the case on Halloween nights, the young boy's wish came true. For as he drifted off to sleep, he heard the sound of a winding horn. In his dream, the young boy stood before the Black Woodsman who sat upon his giant black steed. The specter looked down at the young boy with glowing crimson eyes, which were said to be two coals from the very pits of hell. But this time it was true, the young boy was not afraid. Instead, he stared right back at the Woodsman, his own eyes shining red.

No one in the quaint little town knew what became of the four vile children. They had simply never come home that night. There were those who claimed they had been awakened by screams on the wind. There were those who reported that they had found four pairs of shoes, all reduced to smoking piles of ash. What happened to those wretched other children, the townsfolk would never truly know. But the young boy did. And he knew that in the end, he was in fact, no mouse.

15

The Old Woman in a Basket Redux

There was an old woman tossed up in a basket,
Seventeen times as high as the moon,
Where she was going I did sure ask it,
In her hand she carried a twisted old broom

'Old woman, old woman, old woman' quath I,
O wither, o wither, o wither, so high?
To the Sabbath I travel across the night sky,
Dost thou wish to come with by-and-by?

There was an old woman tossed up in a basket,
Seventeen times as high as the moon,
Where she was going I did sure ask it,
To me she handed the twisted old broom

'Old woman, old woman, old woman' said I,
Please tell, please tell, how do *I* fly?
Close your eyes, believe, and try,
And your spirit will be free by-and-by.

The Farmer's Daughter

The farmer's daughter was, in many ways, a strange girl. Most thought of her as independent, perhaps a bit standoffish. Yet, there were others who felt that the farmer's daughter was uncanny, even frightening.

"There's just something off about that girl," they'd whisper as she passed them by in the market.

The farmer gave no mind to the petty gossip though, for his daughter had proven herself to be dutiful and hardworking. As it had happened, after the passing of his wife, the farmer's land had grown fallow and his cattle had become ill. No matter what he did, his crops would not grow and his herd would not thrive. In a moment when all seemed to be lost, the farmer's daughter walked out the kitchen door, through the flower garden, and disappeared behind the big red barn. After a while she returned and assured her father that everything would be just fine.

And, just as the farmer's daughter had foretold, the land grew green once more and the cattle's health was restored. In fact, from that time on, the farmer always sold out of his produce while at the market. There were those who swore that a soup made from the farmer's vegetables could cure even the nastiest of colds, while a generous serving of his cow's butter had the power to soothe a broken heart. Yet there were also those who were jealous of the farmer and began to whisper that there was something wicked behind his sudden success.

Before long, rumors of Witchery had arisen, with the farmer's daughter suspected of having made a deal with the Devil. The more that the farmer's abundance grew, the more intense the gossip became. There were even those who were so bold as to speak direct warnings to the farmer about his daughter's supposed Witchcraft. But to his credit, the farmer brushed off these warnings, believing them to be nothing more than the product of envy and superstition.

"Besides," he thought to himself, "I spend most of the day working alongside my daughter. I'd know if she were a Witch, would I not?"

However, there are only so many murmurs one can hear before a natural curiosity starts to take hold. Thus, the farmer began to pay closer attention to his daughter, looking for signs that might suggest that she was indeed a Witch. But the only thing he found was what he already knew to be true, that his daughter was a hard worker who cared deeply for her father, for the land, and for the cattle. The only curious thing about the girl was her habit of taking her dinner outside.

As it went, every evening the farmer's daughter would take her plate out the kitchen door, through the flower garden, and disappear behind the big red barn. He never questioned his daughter though, figuring she simply loved being out of doors. He tried hard to let the girl be, but curiosity has a way of latching on and refusing to let go.

"Where does she go? Could she really be a Witch?" These questions now echoed relentlessly through the farmer's mind.

So, one evening, when the farmer's curiosity had finally possessed him fully, he decided to follow his daughter and get to the bottom of the matter once and for all. He watched as she took her plate of food out the kitchen door, through the flower garden, and disappeared behind the big red barn. He went after the girl, sure that he would find her sitting in some pretty spot, innocently enjoying her dinner. However, the farmer could have done nothing to prepare himself for the sight he was about to see.

There, resting against a stone wall was the farmer's daughter. She was not alone though, for on the ground in front of her was a large rattlesnake. But before the farmer could shout in fear for the girl's safety, he watched as she reached forward and offered some of her bread to the serpent.

"Here you are, Mr. Gray-Coat. Won't you please bless my father's land? Won't you please bring health to his cattle?"

The farmer looked on in horror as the snake's tail rattled to and fro in response to his daughter's voice. He knew at that moment that everything the townsfolk had said was true, his daughter was a Witch and here she was with her infernal familiar. As he was not a man to falter in fear, he swiftly grabbed a nearby shovel. In a blinding rage he pushed his daughter to the side and raised the shovel high above his head.

"Father, no!" the girl cried.

But it was too late. The farmer deftly brought down the shovel, cleaving the rattlesnake in two.

19

In the days that followed, the farmer's daughter mysteriously took ill, so much so that soon she was completely bedridden. The girl would not eat nor would she drink, growing thin and pale. All the while she wept for the rattlesnake whom she had called Mr. Gray-Coat. The farmer did his best to ignore his daughter's sobs as he truly believed that she would someday thank him. He had, after all, set her free from the snares of Witchery. Just the same, the girl got worse, as did the farm itself. The crops turned black and moldy and the herd dropped dead one by one.

Exasperated, the farmer came to realize that his abundance had indeed been brought upon by his daughter and the rattlesnake he had so quickly killed. Desperate to regain his good fortune, he went to his daughter's room to beg for forgiveness, to plead for her help once more. Perhaps, he thought, she could summon a new spirit to bless the land and the cattle. But this would never be, for when the farmer approached the bed, he found that his daughter, once so lovely, had wasted away into a hollow husk of a girl. She was dead.

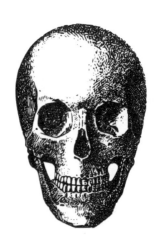

A Most Wicked Malediction

With a candle black and wolfsbane flower, my hex I have begun. By a lock of hair and image grave, you shall become undone. With a sparrow's bone and hangman's rope, your spirit I do bind. By buckthorn's spine and poppy seeds, your psyche I unwind.

With salt that's spilt and a coyote's tooth, misfortune now sets in. By graveyard dirt and a broken cross, no longer can you win. With a shattered mirror and black cat's tail, your luck is at its end. By a rusty blade and henbane leaf, all blessings I do rend.

With the sharpest nails and a chicken's heart, your body starts to ail. By bitter blood and a tanglefoot, your health is soon to fail. With black hen feathers and a death cap shroom, disease begins to seep. By a rattler's venom and hornets' nest, a sickness sets in deep.

With church bell grease and a mayapple root, your fate herein be sealed. By rancid oil and bramble vine, this malediction shall not yield. With jimsonweed and a raven's claw, salvation shant be found. By ashes black and a burial shroud, I put you in the ground.

On the Poisonous Nature of Love

There once was a lonely Witch who longed for nothing more than to be loved. She pined away, day in and day out, for the affections of one man in particular. But, as fate would have it, this man had eyes for someone else. And so, the Witch could do nothing but watch as the man she wanted most became engaged to another.

As time went on the Witch became overcome with jealousy. Her love turned to obsession and it twisted around her heart like rusted barbed wire. She grew nasty and mean, with eyes like fire whenever she saw her beloved walking through town hand-in-hand with his betrothed. Eventually, something within the Witch snapped, like a rotted black stick, and she decided it was time to act.

The Witch had long ago heard of the mandrake's legendary powers to incite love. Perhaps through the root's magical intercession, she could have her heart's wish. In the past, she would have balked at the idea of bewitching another. Love should come naturally, she thought. But things were different now, and she was desperate. Just thinking of the man she yearned for with another woman left her hunched over, gasping for breath, fingernails digging into her palms till drops of blood emerged.

On the day of Venus, the Witch began to work on a philtre that would rouse passionate love within the man. Love that would blaze within him, for her and no one else. Into her cauldron, she emptied a bottle of red wine, so dark that it appeared black. Next, she added copious amounts of honey, the fragrance of which was sweet enough to cause one to swoon on the spot. She sprinkled in rose petals and star anise, stirring in her amorous intentions with clockwise motions. The Witch pricked her left thumb with barely a wince, allowing three droplets of her crimson blood to fall into the brew.

Finally, unraveling a silk cloth, the Witch revealed an old gnarled root. The wizened thing looked humanoid, with arms and legs. She had paid a small fortune for the mandrake and thought to herself how it had better work. Dangling the root above the simmering cauldron she intoned her solemn spell:

Mandrake root, do as I say,
Bring my love to me today,
Instill this brew with my desire,
So that his love will burn like fire.
That he may have no rest nor sleep,
Until he comes to me to speak.

With the last word, the Witch released the mandrake. The potion gave a hiss as the root sank into its scarlet depths. Thick, fragrant plumes of steam rose from the cauldron and wafted out the open window. The Witch's face contorted into a wicked grin, knowing that the love she so frightfully craved would soon be hers.

It took no time at all for the man to arrive at the Witch's door where he knocked feverishly until let inside. The Witch led him into her kitchen, her ravenous grip guiding him to a chair near the hearth. The man spoke no words but instead looked upon the Witch with glassy eyes. He hardly stirred as she handed him a glass filled with the potent love philtre. He made no protest as she brought the glass to his lips and tilted it back.

Almost immediately the dazed look on the man's face was replaced with a wide smile. He now gazed at the Witch with pure adoration. She could hardly believe it, her magic had worked! The man seized her hands and began to speak words of devotion, promising to her his heart, body, and soul. The Witch felt tears brimming in her eyes, this was everything for which she could have hoped.

But as quickly as it had spread across his face, the man's smile vanished. He started with a wretch, clutching his stomach. In horror, the Witch watched as her beloved fell to the floor with a thundering crash. Had she not been so blinded by her jealous need to possess this man, the Witch would have realized that at the same time, mandrake can bestow love, when ingested it also acts as a powerful poison. Now she could only stare helplessly as the man she loved succumbed to the agonizing throes of death.

For years after, the Witch would visit the man's grave. She would bring no flowers, only the hard lesson she had learned. For it was only when she saw the man's lifeless eyes that she understood the ways in which love can be a sickness, a sweet, saccharin poison not unlike the mandrake's own. And now she knew that if left unchecked, love itself could easily drive someone utterly insane. It could cause the ruination of the very person you so deliriously desired.

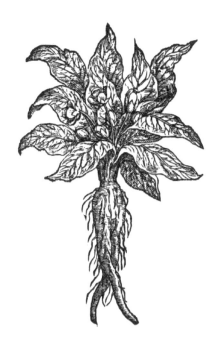

Blåkulla

Act I

At midnight we did go,
Dance the crossroad just so,
And the devil then appeared.
On his beasts we did fly,
Over churches so high,
For Blåkulla we all had steered.

Act II

A meadow with no end,
Is where we did descend,
Blåkulla! Was our raucous cry.
In the center of it,
A great big house did sit,
Underneath a starless sky.

Act III

With our blood we did write,
In a black book that night,
Twas our souls that we did sell.
Then to be born anew,
In some water we threw,
Shavings of an old church bell.

Act IV
Once Witches we were made,
A fine feast was then laid,
We supped on cheese and on bread,
In a dance we next tore,
We cursed and we swore,
The devil then brought us to bed.

Pyewacket

There was once a Witch who, feeling quite lonely, decided to seek out a familiar spirit. To do so, she went on the night of a full moon to the edge of a rushing river. With a determined voice, she spoke:

Hickety pickety, hickety pickety,
Where can my familiar be?
Are you in the sky above or down below the sea?
Hickety pickety, hickety pickety,
Can you hear my call to thee?
Be you far or be you near, familiar come to me.

In response to the Witch's intonation, a breeze swept through the tall pine trees and across her brow. She knew it would only be a matter of time before her call was answered.

And answered it was.

On the third night after the summoning, the Witch was surprised by the sudden appearance of a spirit in her bedroom. She had been preparing for sleep when the specter materialized, first as shadowy, gray smoke and then as a small, translucent cat.

Hardly able to contain her excitement, the Witch greeted the spirit and asked, "Have you perchance come to be my familiar?"

"Why, yes. I have." replied the spirit in a whispery voice.

"Oh, how marvelous! What is your name?"

"Pyewacket." he answered.

"It's very nice to meet you Pyewacket," the Witch said politely. "Please, tell me, what can we do together?"

"Together we can do powerful magic! But for now, I am tired from my long journey across the spirit world. Won't you give me an offering?" Pyewacket asked with a great yawn.

"Certainly. Would you like some milk? Or how about some honey?"

"No, no. That won't do. Why don't you just go to sleep and I will help myself?" he replied.

Although she had many questions for her new familiar, the Witch thought it best to take heed of the spirit's request. And so, she lay her head down upon her pillow and drifted off to sleep.

In the morning the Witch awoke with a slight pain in her left shoulder. Pulling up the sleeve of her nightgown, she discovered two small, red bumps. But her mind was too preoccupied with thoughts of Pyewacket to pay much attention to the minor affliction. Instead, she wondered where her new familiar had gone.

To the Witch's dismay, Pyewacket was nowhere to be found. The day passed by and it was only after the sun had set and the moon had risen that the spirit returned, first as shadowy, gray smoke and then as a small, translucent cat.

"Pyewacket!" cried the Witch. "I thought you had abandoned me."

"No, no, silly Witch. I am your familiar! I would not abandon you."

"But you were gone for so long!" bemoaned the Witch.

"Of course, I was! I have other things to do, you know? You must be patient." Pyewacket chided.

"But..." The Witch began to speak.

"You must give me time to adjust." Pyewacket interrupted. "Now, go to sleep and I will help myself to another offering. Perhaps tomorrow we will get to work."

Although she still had many questions for her new familiar, the Witch was also afraid of offending the spirit. And so, she lay her head down upon her pillow and drifted off to sleep.

In the morning the Witch awoke with greater pain in her left shoulder. Pulling up the sleeve of her nightgown she discovered the two red bumps were now raw and cracking open. But again, she was too enthralled with the prospect of working magic with Pyewacket to give much thought to the matter.

31

As before, and to the Witch's extreme disappointment, the day passed by without Pyewacket's presence. When the sun had set and the moon had risen, the spirit appeared, first as shadowy, gray smoke and then as a small, translucent cat.

"Pyewacket, there you are!" the Witch said, slightly annoyed. "Where have you been all day?"

"As I've said, I have much to do." the spirit retorted. "If you want me to stay longer in this world you must build me a house in which to live."

"I'm sorry, I hadn't realized you needed a house!" the Witch apologized, feeling quite foolish.

"Clearly not." Pyewacket said curtly. "Now, go to sleep and I will help myself to another offering. Tomorrow, you will build me a house, and then we can get to work."

Despite the deep longing she'd had for a magical companion, the Witch couldn't help but feel that something was amiss with her new familiar. And so, as she lay her head down upon her pillow, she only pretended to drift off to sleep. Before long, the Witch felt something jump up onto her bed. She kept her eyes closed as it crawled closer and closer toward her.

Without warning, there was a heavy weight upon the Witch's chest. Cautiously, she peeked from behind her eyelids. In the light of the moon, she saw Pyewacket's feline form upon her. She was about to speak out when, all at once, the spectral cat bit down upon her left shoulder. The Witch screamed, sitting bolt upright. She clutched her shoulder and looked wildly about the room, but Pyewacket had vanished.

The Witch did not sleep a wink the rest of the night. In the morning she applied cider vinegar and a soothing balm to her shoulder, understanding now that it was her blood that Pyewacket had been helping himself to. She knew then that the spirit she had so unquestioningly let into her life had no real interest in being her familiar at all.

Devising a plan, the Witch sought out a sturdy wooden box to serve as a house for the duplicitous spirit. When the sun had set and the moon had risen, Pyewacket appeared, first as shadowy, gray smoke and then as a small, translucent cat.

"Hello Pyewacket," greeted the Witch, feigning sweetness. "I have procured a house for you as requested."

"I suppose this will do," Pyewacket said, sniffing at the box.

"Oh, but you must climb inside, I've filled it with the softest of linens, just for you." said the Witch, lifting the lid to reveal the folds of colorful cloth within.

With a huff, Pyewacket assumed his smoky form and drifted into the box to inspect its contents. Quickly, the Witch slammed the lid shut, trapping the spirit inside.

"Let me out!" Pyewacket demanded angrily.

"No! You have lied to me. You are no familiar spirit but a devious interloper and now you must go!" The Witch decreed.

"You simpleton! Let me out this instant!" was the spirit's reply.

The box shook violently as the Witch took hold of it and ran over to the blazing hearth. Without a moment of hesitation, she threw it into the fire along with a fistful of blessed salt. The spirit shrieked from within his burning prison. Undeterred, the Witch spoke:

In nomine Patris et Filii, et Spiritus Sancti,
Ashes to ashes, dust to dust!

All at once the cries stopped and everything was silent. By morning the box had been reduced to cinders and the foul trickster Pyewacket was no more.

The Confession of Agnes Sampson

Ah yes, my good King, please sit down for a spell,
If you want my confession, you best listen well.
For a Witch you have caught, this much might be true,
But true fear you know not till my story is through.

On Hallows Eve last our dear Devil did call,
For Witches to gather, a great many in all.
To the sea we took, in sieves we did sail,
The water was dark then and the moon, it was pale.

At North Berwick kirk, we did finally land,
We danced through the old graves, all linked hand in
hand.
It was Fian who led with the greatest of zeal,
As merrily we spun round to Gilly's gay reel.

Next into the kirk we did walk by-and-by,
Our great Master was there in the pulpit up high.
We paid our respects and then all of our dues,
Before the Devil did speak and give us the news.

The King is our enemy, that's what he said,
And see to it we must that quite soon you be dead.
So, with murderous intent, plans did we hatch,
With the most wicked of arts, your life we'd dispatch.

So, a big black toad I firstly did gather,
It's poison I thought, on your linens I'd slather.
But some fabric of yours, I could not attain,
Thus was I stopped from ending your earthly life's reign.

But worry not my King, we did try once more,
Upon you and your bride as you left Denmark's shore.
We summoned a storm, drowned a cat in the sea,
It was our hope that soon in its place you would be.

Sadly, we did fail, as alive here you sit,
But mistaken you be if you think we will quit.
We Witches shall not stop, to plot and conspire,
Until at last my good king, you do so expire.

Still, I see in your face, my story you doubt,
But I am no liar, so my powers I'll tout.
So now lean in close and do lend me your ear,
And the wedding night words from the Queen you will
hear...

Escape of the Witch-Hare

There was once a young man who, after leaving his family
home, had come to be employed on a small dairy farm.
The owner of the farm was a kindly old man who had
come from a long line of stockmen. The young man took
quickly to his work, spending long days milking and
otherwise tending to the cows. The farmer was impressed
with the young man's skill, a fact which the latter relished,
for he was as prideful as he was hardworking.

Well, one night, a terrible storm blew in across the land.
The rain pelted the earth angrily and thunder shook the
heavens above. Worrying about the cattle out in the barn,
the young man went out to check on them. He rushed
across the farm and entered the dark barn with only a
small lantern for light. Right away he was struck by how
eerily silent the barn was, with not a sound coming from
the cows. In addition to their silence, the young man
noticed how the herd stood frozen in place as if entranced.

The young man walked through the barn, looking for
what could possibly be causing the cattle's strange
behavior. Shining the lantern's light close to the ground,
he couldn't believe his eyes. There, underneath one of the
cows was a large hare suckling from the udders. In
surprise, the young man let out a shout. Instantly, the hare
ran off. The young man tried to chase the creature but it
disappeared out the barn door and into the stormy night.

The young man dashed back to the house, through the pelting rain, to tell the farmer about what he had just seen. But instead of sharing in his alarm, the farmer burst out laughing. He quieted the young man and sat him down near the fire to dry off.

"Now look here, I'm going to explain to you what my daddy explained to me and what his daddy explained to him," the farmer began. "There is a very old Witch who lives in these parts..."

"A Witch!" interrupted the young man in exclamation.

"Yes boy, a shapeshifting Witch. Well as it was, back in the day, she wreaked havoc on this farm, sucking those cows dry. All in the shape of a hare. One day, my granddaddy shot that hare right in the leg. He pursued the injured critter all the way up the mountain yonder. Well, at the very top, he found the Witch cowering in a little shack, a great big hole in her leg. She begged him not to kill her and promised that she wouldn't bother the farm no more."

"What did your granddaddy do?" asked the young man.

"My granddaddy was not a forgiving man, but he sure was slick. So, he proposed that if the Witch would bestow her blessing upon the farm, she could continue to take a share. And so, a truce was struck. My family has honored that deal to this day, and our farm has prospered."

"You can't be serious! Witches aren't real!" the young man said incredulously.

"Witches are real, boy, whether you believe in them or not. And if you see that hare again, you best leave it be." the farmer warned.

The young man went to bed that night, unable to get the farmer's story out of his mind. He refused to believe that it was a Witch he had seen in the barn. While he had certainly never heard of a hare suckling a cow, he reasoned that perhaps the creature was diseased. And if that was the case, it needed to be put down in order to protect the herd.

By morning the storm had not yet broken. Outside the ground was flooded and muddy while the sky remained a sea of roiling black clouds. The young man went out to the barn to take care of the cattle and he stayed there for the remainder of the day, a shotgun slung over his shoulder. He wanted to be ready if the hare returned, resolute to wait as long as it took. And, as it would turn out, his wait was not long.

As lightning flashed and thunder echoed outside, the hare hopped right on into the barn. The young man was surprised by the animal's confidence as it approached the cows, seemingly ignoring his presence. Slowly, the young man positioned himself and took aim at the hare. The wind beat the sides of the barn relentlessly as he put his finger on the trigger. It was at that moment that the hare looked up and directly at the young man. For a moment all was still, as their four eyes locked upon one another.

BANG!

Having heard the gunshot, the farmer hobbled as quickly as he could through the wind and the rain. When he entered the barn, he could only sigh at the scene before him. The young man was sprawled dead on the blood-soaked ground. Nearby lay his shotgun, the back blown clean off and still smoking. And sitting there, looking at it all with big eyes and a twitching nose was the Witch Hare.

"I told him to leave you be." The farmer said, shaking his head sadly.

A Most Fortuitous Blessing

With a candle white and a sprig of mint, this spell I do
begin. By rabbit's foot and mercury dime, good fortune is
yours to win. With an orange's peel and bumble bee,
success you'll surely gain. By four-leaf clover and toad
bone ring, fast luck you will attain.

With a thread of blue and holey stone, may health be on
your side. By olive oil and a snakeskin shed, great blessings
shall be betide. With holy water and a clootie charm,
cured you are of ills. By plantain leaf and a mussel shell,
with strength your body fills.

With an oaken branch and crimson star, protected you
now be. By pickling salt and a horse's shoe, from danger
you're set free. With iron ore and a skeleton key, enemies
can't come near. By rosemary bunch and a trusted broom,
banished be all fear.

With roses red and silver bells, sweet love you'll always
find. By goose's feather and honeycomb, may friends be
loyal and kind. With a heart shaped rock and mourning
dove, true family does abound. By lavender buds and worn
hearthstone, do peace and love surround.

Dance of the Elfame Queen

There was once a man who, reluctantly walking home, had decided to cut across an expansive field. The sun had already descended below the horizon and the purple sky was awash with twinkling stars. Tired from his long day's work, the man walked sluggishly through the freshly planted rows of beans. But while the twilight world around him was still and silent, his mind was not.

As of late, the man's life had been plagued with vexation and apathy. He was tired of working, he was tired of providing for his family. He no longer wanted to be a husband. He no longer wanted to be a father. He felt burdened by all of his responsibilities. If only he could relinquish them, then he could do as he pleased. The man wished to get away from his family, to be forever free.

Suddenly pulled from his discontent, the man noticed the sound of tinkling bells coming from up ahead. The sound was soft and ethereal, instantly soothing his frayed nerves. Whereas before his pace was slow and hesitant, the man now walked faster, drawn to the beautiful sound.

As he approached the middle of the field, the man let out a gasp. The scene before him was one of pure enchantment. The ground here had erupted with foxgloves, hyacinths, and primrose. The sound of bells was joined by the music of a harp. In the center of it, all was a wide circle of fat, red-capped mushrooms. Within the circle stood a tall, slender woman dressed in a mossy green gown. Her long, dark hair was topped with an elegant silver crown that dazzled like the stars above.

The mysterious woman beckoned the man forward, pulling him towards her with a mere look. Entranced, he stepped into the circle of mushrooms. He gazed into the woman's emerald eyes as she took his hands. The music grew louder as they began to dance, slow and steady while the moon ascended in the sky.

The man found himself enraptured by the eldritch woman. In her strong embrace, he felt his worries melt away. No longer did he care about his work, nor his husband, nor his children. His only thoughts were dedicated to the freedom he felt in the moment, spinning round the mushroom circle.

"Who are you?" The man finally asked, surprised to find his voice shaking.

"I am the Elfame Queen. I heard your wishes. To get away. To be forever free. And now you shall." Her voice was deep and her words melodious.

And so, they spun on and on, around and around. The flowers, the stars, and the harp all twirling together in ecstasy. The man continued to stare into the verdant depths of the Queen's eyes, reveling in the joy that filled his heart.

"Are you ready to leave your life behind?" The Queen asked.

"Yes." replied the man.

"What about your home?" She asked.

"It means nothing to me." He replied.

"What about your family?" Asked the Queen.

"They mean nothing to me." Replied the man.

The Queen smiled and the man watched as her eyes narrowed. The music's tempo picked up speed then and so did their dance. At first, the man laughed as they capered about. But before long he began to tire, finding himself short of breath.

"Please, let us take a rest." The man said to the Queen but she only stared at him with the same smile and narrowed eyes.

"Please!" He said once again, this time with more urgency. His legs were worn-out and his feet were sore. He tried to break free from the Queen but she grabbed his wrists and refused to let go.

Faster and faster they danced. The starlight became blinding. The scent of the flowers became overbearing. The harp's music became disorienting. Gone was the sense of peaceful calm, replaced by a mad and inescapable frenzy.

The man's knees buckled and his lungs burned inside his chest. He struggled against the Queen's grip, blood oozing from where her nails dug into his flesh. Tears filled the man's eyes as he remembered the family he had so carelessly wished away.

"Please! I want to go home!" The man begged.

45

But he would never go home again. In the morning, a farmer discovered the man's lifeless body in the field. Gone were the mushrooms. Gone were the tinkling bells. Gone were the man's toes, which had been danced clean off.

The Nightshade's Revenge

Silly boy, carelessly plucking my shiny eyes black,
You took without asking, you gave nothing back.
My powers you thought, could be yours just the same,
A daft little fool playing a dangerous game.

To fly far away, you so desperately desired,
But it was your undoing that I had conspired.
See, shortcuts are useless when you have no skill,
Especially those with a strong penchant to kill.

Yet you still slathered me on as a green ointment thick,
You drank me down thinking that would do the trick.
But disrespect begets this wicked Queen's wrath,
Prepared you were not for this most poisonous path.

With such little heed, you placed your life's fate in my
hand,
You believed my spirit was yours to command.
But with pupils wide, you knew all was not well,
Your chest heaved in agony with your heartbeat's swell.

You fell to your knees and you wretched upon the ground,
You screamed out in anguish but yet made no sound.
From your pretty pink lungs, I took all the air,
Your demise was imminent, it was only fair.

I let out a big laugh, you had but yourself to blame,
So stupid and arrogant, oh what a shame.
You thought me inert, dominion you assumed,
You thought wrong silly boy, and your soul I consumed.

There you lay on the floorboards, body stiff as a stone,
No one could help, you were completely alone.
With one final gasp, you did finally die,
You got your wish then, away your spirit could fly.

Frau Perchta

There once was a mother who had two children, a boy and a girl. The mother was a kindhearted woman who worked hard to provide for her children. The boy and girl on the other hand were lazy and demanding. While their mother cooked and cleaned, the boy and girl sat idly about, lifting not a finger to help. But the mother loved her children dearly, and so she never complained, she simply encouraged them to do their share.

As it went, it was a particularly frigid winter. The mother had worked hard to finish her spinning, toiling away through the night. She intended to use her earnings to provide her children with extra Christmas gifts. The boy and girl had been especially cantankerous and it was the mother's hope that these presents would improve their temperament.

But alas, come Christmas morning, the children lamented over their gifts.

"What good is this?" the boy cried, tossing down one of his new toys.

"This isn't what I wanted!" exclaimed the girl in disgust, looking down at an unwrapped present.

The mother was distraught over her children's dissatisfaction.

"Please children, be kind! I worked hard for those gifts."

But the children would not be calm, and they certainly would not be kind. Instead, they set about throwing a tantrum.

"Remember children," the mother said, with a slight firmness in her voice, "Frau Perchta will punish the misbehaved."

The children rolled their eyes at the mention of Frau Perchta. They knew the story well, of the beak-nosed woman who came to town on Twelfth Night. Frau Perchta was said to visit homes, looking to see that everything was neat and tidy and that all the spinning had been done. If she found a home to be satisfactory, she would bestow her blessings. However, if she found the home to be in disrepair, she would swiftly destroy everything inside.

"Well then, you had better make sure the house is clean!" the children taunted.

The mother just sighed for she knew that her beloved children were missing the point. For Frau Perchta's proclivities included acts much more frightening than vandalism.

And so, Twelfth Night came and the mother prepared the house for Frau Perchta's visit. She swept the floors, washed the dishes, and finished her spinning. The entire time she encouraged her children to help out, but they would hear nothing of it.

"Leave us alone!" cried the boy.

"We're busy!" exclaimed the girl.

The mother sighed and continued her work. And as the sun dipped low in the sky, the children continued to misbehave.

"Please children, be kind! Remember, Frau Perchta comes tonight." The mother chided.

"Oh mother, we don't believe in that silly old story," retorted the boy.

"We will do as we please!" snapped the girl.

As the moon rose high in the east, the mother finished her preparations. She set the table with shortbread cookies, blackberry jam, and spice cake. The food was an offering to Frau Perchta and the *heimchen*, the band of restless spirits who followed her.

Finally, the mother tried to tuck her beloved children into their beds. But of course, the boy and girl put up a fight and bemoaned that they were not at all sleepy. And the mother, who at this point was very tired, shouted, "Get to sleep now! Or Frau Perchta will get you!"

Shocked by their mother's unusual outburst, the children complied and crawled into their beds. The mother herself was surprised by her children's obedience.

But of course, the children were only pretending to listen. For once their mother had closed the door to her room, they crept from their beds and down the stairs. Giggling, the boy and girl sat themselves down at the table.

"Silly mother, leaving these treats out," laughed the boy.

"We might as well eat them ourselves!" snickered the girl.

And so, they stuffed their faces with the cookies and jam and cake which had been meant to appease Frau Perchta and the heimchin.

Creeeeeak.

"What was that?" asked the boy, his lips stained purple from the jam.

"Just the wind in the trees," assured the girl, helping herself to more cake.

But it was not the wind in the trees. The children had been so distracted by the treats that they failed to notice the front door slowly swinging open.

Skrskrskr

"What was that?" asked the boy, munching on yet another cookie.

"Just mice under the floor," assured the girl, stuffing more food in her mouth.

But it was not mice under the floor. Again, the children had been so distracted by the treats that they failed to notice the beak-nosed woman walking towards them, her long toenails scratching the wooden floor.

Grrrrrr.

"What was that?" Asked the boy, licking his fingers.

"Just the furnace kicking on," assured the girl, finishing off the cake.

But it was not the furnace kicking on. Unfortunately, the children had continued to be so distracted by the treats that they were much too late in noticing as Frau Perchta came down upon them.

In the morning the mother came down the stairs, having had a restful sleep. Sunlight streamed through the windows, casting everything in a warm, golden glow. Including her beloved children who were sitting still and silent at the table. At first, she was astonished that her children were so calm, especially given the early morning hour. But as she drew closer to the table, she quickly understood the cause of their sudden passivity.

As was Frau Perchta's way, the children's stomachs had been cut open and scooped clean out, their viscera replaced with copious amounts of trash. The mother sat down at the table, looking across at her children who were finally behaving. She let out a long sigh and she smiled.

"Thank you, Frau."

All Them Witches

All them Witches, all them Witches, taking to the sky.
Upon their brooms, upon their sticks, through the night
they fly.

All them Witches, all them Witches, speak unholy vows.
To their master, to the Devil, do they lowly bow.

All them Witches, all them Witches, feasting at the table.
Drinking wine, eating bread, as much as they are able.

All them Witches, all them Witches, dancing in a ring. A
jaunty song, an eerie song, does the coven sing.

All them Witches, all them Witches, pair off one by one.
In the shadows, in the grass, they have flirtatious fun.

All them Witches, all them Witches, away they all do run.
With the coming, with the rising, of the morning sun.

Black Shuck

One day, some time ago, there was a Witch out collecting herbs. Humming a little song, they happily walked along a path that snaked between two steep hills. It was a special trail that the Witch frequently visited in order to gather yarrow and bee balm, along with blue vervain and St. John's wort.

Although the Witch was cheerful as they wandered the valley, the weather did not reflect their bright disposition. The sun was hidden behind thick clouds, clouds which had rapidly started to darken. Still, the Witch continued their leisurely stroll. In fact, they were in such deep reverie that they failed to detect just how bad the weather had become.

It was only when the first heavy drops of rain began to fall that the Witch noticed the gloomy change in the atmosphere. And so, they reluctantly threw up their hood, grabbed their basket of herbs, and made a start for home. By now though, the wind had picked up and thunder rumbled ominously overhead.

Without warning, it started to downpour. The sheets of rain fell with such intensity that it quickly became difficult to see. Lightning flashed across the sky as the Witch hastened their pace, a sense of urgency flooding their consciousness.

Aroooooooooooo.

The Witch stopped dead in their tracks at the sudden sound of a dog baying loudly in the distance.

Aroooooooooooo.

Even through the claps of thunder, the haunting call was unmistakable. Shivers ran up the Witch's spine. There had long been stories regarding a monstrous black dog who prowled the valley when storms rolled in. It was said that anyone who was unfortunate enough to get caught outside during such weather would surely fall victim to the frightful canine.

Arooooooooooo.

The Witch stood frozen in fear as the baying grew closer. They knew in their bones that they were in danger, that they were now the hound's intended prey.

Arooooooooooo.

With great effort, the Witch broke free from their stasis and began to run, dropping their basket of herbs to the muddy ground.

Grrrrrrrrrrrr.

The howling sound had turned to a snarl as it drew near. The Witch raced faster, wind and rain slapping against their face, stinging their eyes.

Grrrrrrrrrrrr.

Braving a quick glance over their shoulder, the Witch let out a scream. In the darkness of the night blazed a pair of fiery red eyes.

Grrrrrrrrrrrr.

Faster and faster the Witch went, still they could feel the big black dog at their heels. Flashes of lightning illuminated the hills on either side of the steep valley. Hopelessness seeped into the Witch's heart as they gasped for breath and clutched their side.

Grrrrrrrrrr.

Just when all seemed to be lost, the Witch spotted the welcoming light of the main road up ahead. Remembering that travelers were safe from the big black dog once outside of the valley, they bolted forward ignoring the burning in their lungs.

And finally, with a sigh of relief, the Witch touched down upon the paved road. Daring once more to look behind them, they turned around. But nothing was there except the darkness and the rain. The big black dog had vanished.

By morning the storm had passed and the birds were singing in the trees once more. But despite the calm, the Witch found themselves unsettled. For as it turned out, during the night's downpour there had been a massive landslide in the valley. The little winding path had been completely devoured by rock and by mud. Still thinking about the devilish hound that had chased them, the Witch was left wondering. Was the dog trying to hunt them down? Or drive them out of harm's way?

Ode to Nicnevin

Witch Mother Nicnevin,
Fair daughter of Heaven,
I praise your ancient name,
Weaver of fate,
With powers so great,
Queen of lovely Elfame.

Witch Mother Nicnevin,
Dark daughter of Heaven,
I honor your old shade,
Mistress of bones,
Oh, shaper of stones,
Head of Hallowmass Rade.

Witch Mother Nicnevin,
Wise daughter of Heaven,
I bless your eldritch heart,
Caster of clew,
Of magic spells too,
Guide in sorcerous art.

The Witch's Ghost

There was once a Witch with a troubled soul who, in her desire to leave her sorrows behind, moved far away from the home she once knew. She wandered for quite some time, trying her best to escape the painful memories that clawed at her heart. Her journey was long and arduous, with the days and nights passing by, one after the other.

But eventually, after what felt like an entire lifetime, the Witch found herself a new home. It was an old house in an old town on a rocky coastline. She was drawn to the house, as if by some magnetic force that she couldn't quite explain. And so, she quickly settled in.

The Witch went to sleep that first night feeling a sense of relief, believing that her hardships were finally at an end. Perhaps here, in this house, she would at long last be free from the past which had haunted her so relentlessly.

She was wrong.

The first night brought with it a cold draft. The Witch awoke, shivering and clutching at her blankets. Her breath emerged in icy plumes from between her chattering teeth. Perhaps a window had been left open, she thought. But this was not the case as each one was found shut tight.

Walking back to her bed, through the chilly darkness, the Witch couldn't shake the sense of unease. Something was not right in her house.

On the second day, the Witch got to work, for she would not allow her new life to be threatened by some lingering presence. She placed bowls of pickling salt around the house and burned frankincense, juniper, and rosemary. She clanged bells and covered the mirrors with black cloth.

But on the second night, the noises began. Again, the Witch found herself awakened by a cold draft but now she also heard scratches at the door. It was as if an animal were trying to claw its way into her bedroom. At first, these scratches were soft, barely even audible. However, as the Witch sat up in bed the noises became more desperate, violent.

The Witch got out of bed and tiptoed to the door with bated breath. The scratching was now so intense that the door itself was vibrating on its hinges. The Witch reached towards the doorknob with trembling hands. Grabbing hold of the knob, she steeled herself. Her heart was racing, beating rapidly against her chest. But just as she was about to yank the door open the scratching ceased. The room was plunged into a deafening silence.

BANG!

The Witch jumped back, falling to the cold wooden floor. *BANG! BANG!* The sounds of ghostly fists pounded against the door. *BANG! BANG! BANG!* The force of the sounds reverberated through the entire room. The Witch crawled away from the door, too shaken to stand. *BANG! BANG! BANG!*

"What do you want?" She screamed.

BANG! BANG! BANG! A crack appeared in the center of the door, splintering from the intensity of the spectral blows.

"What do you want?" the Witch cried out once more, tears brimming her eyes.

The noises stopped.

On the third day, the Witch pulled out an old grimoire, looking for a way to banish the restless spirit whose behavior only seemed to be escalating. The ritual she found was quite simple in nature, but she hoped that it would be enough.

On four squares of parchment, the Witch wrote, in red ink:

Omnis spiritus laudet Dominum: Mosen habent & prophetas: Exurgat Deus et dissipentur inimici ejus.

Speaking the written words with conviction, she hung each of the squares in the furthest corners of the house.

But on the third night, the Witch woke once more to the cold draft and the scratching at the door. She jumped from her bed, her heart sinking with the realization that her earlier work had been for naught.

BANG! BANG! BANG!

Gritting her teeth, the Witch ran forward and ripped the door open. The hallway was dark and empty. Squinting into the inky blackness, she thought she could make out the shape of someone lurking in the shadows.

"Hello?" The Witch called out.

WHOOSH! A blast of frigid wind shot down the hallway, sending framed pictures smashing to the floor. The Witch's hair billowed behind her as she ran against the gust, stepping over shards of glass. The doors in the hallway opened and slammed shut. *BANG! BANG! BANG!*

All around the house, objects were being tossed about by invisible hands. A lamp shattered against the living room wall as books were torn to shreds in midair. With determination, the Witch made it to the kitchen, flinging the door closed behind her. She could think of only one more ritual to perform. It was her only hope.

Making quick work, the Witch pulled from the cabinets a canister of salt and three black candles. She formed a triangle with the salt, placing a candle at each point. With the candles lit, she formed a circle of salt around herself.

BANG! BANG! BANG! Outside the kitchen, the destruction continued. The Witch braced herself and spoke the words of an old evocation.

By the mysteries of the deep, by the flames of Banal, *by the power of the East, and the silence of the night, by the holy rites of Hecate, I conjure and exorcise thee thou distressed Spirit, to present thy self here, and reveal unto me the cause of thy Calamity, why thou didst offer me violence, where thou art now in being, and where thou wilt hereafter be!*

The cacophony of sounds outside the kitchen stopped and for a brief moment, all was still.

But then, within the triangle of candles and salt, smoke began to coil up from the ground. It grew into an undulating cloud, black as pitch and with an oily sheen. The Witch held her breath as the smoke continued to take shape. The candle flames shot up, wavering wildly. Shadows danced in a frenzy upon the walls.

A figure started to emerge from the smoke, details slowly coming into focus. The deathly silence continued to offer an unrelenting sense of suffocation. The Witch clenched her fists and gnashed her teeth, any moment now she would know the cause of her grief.

And finally, with an unearthly moan, the spirit revealed itself to her. The Witch let out a cry as she looked into the eyes of the ghost that stood before her.

They were her own.

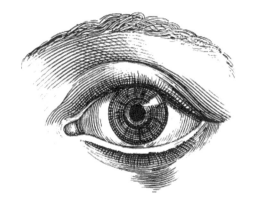

Notes

The Compass Quest
The imagery within this poem is based on Robert
Cochrane's writing - specifically, a document
sent to Norman Gills in March of 1966. In this
document, Cochrane discusses four gods who
each rule an element and reside within a
directional castle. More information can be
found by visiting
http://www.1734-witchcraft.org/gillsthree.html

The Greedy-Hearted Witch
This story is based on Shel Silverstein's book *The
Giving Tree* (1964). I have always despised this
book for the ways in which it glorifies unbridled
self-sacrifice as a form of love. So, in hopes of
promoting healthy boundary setting, I wrote my
own variation of the story.

The Halloween Hunt
The story of *The Halloween Hunt* combines
several folkloric motifs. First is the character of
the Black Woodsman which comes from a story
of the same name told by Hubert J. Davis in his
book *The Silver Bullet* (1975) - which itself is
inspired by Washington Irving's short story *The
Devil and Tom Walker* (1824). Second is the
wider concept of the Wild Hunt and similar tales
about spectral huntsmen.

The Old Woman in a Basket Redux
This particular poem is a reworking of my
favorite nursery rhyme *There was an Old Woman*
(as it is titled in the nursery rhyme book from my
childhood). There have been several variations of
this poem regarding a woman with a broom in a
basket. Perhaps one of the earliest recorded
versions can be found in the preface of *Mother
Goose's Melody; or Sonnets for the Cradle* (1780).

The Farmer's Daughter
The story of *The Farmer's Daughter* is based on a
short folktale found in Clifton Johnson's *What
They Say in New England* (1896). The original
tale does not speak of Witchcraft or familiars, but
I've always wondered what secrets were hiding
between the lines. A truncated version of *The
Farmer's Daughter* can be found in the
companion book I wrote for the Traditional
Witch's Deck (illustrated by Maggie Elram).

On the Poisonous Nature of Love
Mandrake (*Mandragora officinarum*) has long
been reputed to have great magical virtues,
including those pertaining to love. For example,
in the biblical *Song of Solomon*, the young woman
Shulammite brings her love-interest to the
countryside where mandrakes grow. There, the
aroma of the plant induces deep feelings of
adoration within the man. Although mandrake
features in many antiquated love spells and
potions, it's important to remember that the plant
is toxic and should never be ingested.

Additionally, part of the incantation used in this story (*...that he may have no rest nor sleep, until he comes to me to speak...*) comes from several recorded folk charms. Examples of these charms can be found in Graham King's *The British Book of Spells and Charms* (2016).

A truncated version of *On the Poisonous Nature of Love* can be found in the companion book I wrote for the Traditional Witch's Deck (illustrated by Maggie Elram).

Blåkulla
Blåkulla is the name of the place where Swedish Witches were said to gather for their Sabbaths. The specific details in this poem come from the confessions of accused Witches in Mora, Sweden as recorded in Anthony Hornek's contribution to later editions of *Saducismus Triumphatus* (Joseph Glanvill, 1681).

Pyewacket
Pyewacket was one of the names of the familiar spirits belonging to a woman accused of Witchcraft by the infamous Matthew Hopkins in 1644. In his account, Hopkins only describes Pyewacket as an imp. However, Pyewacket has often been used as a name for a Witch's cat in various media such as in the movie *Bell, Book and Candle* (1958).

While rare, there are folkloric accounts of individuals seeking to be rid of familiar spirits. Often it is the case that these spirits are unwillingly gifted or inherited from a dying Witch.

The Confession of Agnes Sampson
Agnes Sampson was an accused Witch from North
Berwick, Scotland. She gave her confession before King
James VI (later to become King James I of England) in
1590. After hearing her confession, the King declared that
Sampson was a liar. Oddly, Sampson decided to prove
herself as a Witch by whispering in the King's ear the
secret words his wife had said to him on their wedding
night. Details of her confession can be found in both
Robert Pitcairn's *Ancient Criminal Trials in Scotland Vol. 1*
(1833) and the pamphlet *Newes From Scotland* published
in 1591.

Escape of the Witch-Hare
Escape of the Witch-Hare is based on the common
folkloric motif of the injured, shapeshifting Witch. Stories
that contain this motif, which can be found all throughout
Europe and North America, follow a pattern in which the
animal is injured (usually shot by a silver bullet), with the
Witch later found with a matching injury. A great example
of such a tale in American folklore is the story of Peg
Wesson which can be found in Ednah Dow Cheney's
Stories of the Olden Times (1890).

Dance of the Elfame Queen
The Queen of Elfame comes from Scottish Witch trial
folklore. She is first mentioned by Bessie Dunlop, who
confessed in 1576 that she had met the Queen of Elfame.
In his transcription of Dunlop's confession, Robert
Pitcairn notes that Elfame refers to the Good Neighbors
or faeries. The Queen later appears in the confessions of
Alison Pearson (1588) and Andro Man (1598).

Frau Perchta

Originating in the upper Germanic Alpine region, Frau Perchta is said to roam during the twelve days between Christmas and Epiphany. Per folklore, she punishes those who have not finished their spinning as well as misbehaved children. In the case of the latter, she slits their stomach open and removes their viscera before filling them with straw or garbage.

Perchta was also believed to have a beautiful side and is related to Holda, another Germanic folk spirit. As such, Perchta was capable of bestowing blessings and was also the caretaker of the *heimchen* who were the spirits of children who died during infancy.

All Them Witches

The title of this poem, and that of this volume is inspired by the film Rosemary's Baby (1968), which itself is based on the novel of the same name by Ira Levin (1967). In the film, as in the novel, the titular character reads from a book entitled *All of Them Witches,* written by the fictional J.R. Hanslet.

Black Shuck

While the dog in this story is not given the specific name, he was inspired by Black Shuck. In East Anglian folklore, Shuck is a spectral dog said to prowl the countryside. As per the lore, Shuck is morally ambivalent and is said to attack travelers or protect them as he sees fit.

Ode to Nicnevin
In Scottish folklore, Nicnevin is a goddess or spirit described by Sir Walter Scot in his *Letters on Demonology and Witchcraft* (1830) as a hag riding upon storms. Scot further notes that Nicnevin is the leader of Witches and faeries. Further information regarding Nicnvein can be found in my book *The Crooked Path: An Introduction to Traditional Witchcraft* (2020).

The Witch's Ghost
Both the paper charm and the exorcism incantation in this story are taken from Reginald Scot's *The Discoverie of Witchcraft* (1584).

About the Author

Kelden has been practicing Traditional Witchcraft for more than a decade. He is the author of *The Crooked Path: An Introduction to Traditional Witchcraft* and *The Witches' Sabbath: An Exploration of History, Folklore, and Modern Practice*. Additionally, his writing has appeared in *The Witch's Altar*, *The New Aradia: A Witch's Handbook to Magical Resistance*, and *This Witch* magazine. Kelden is also the cocreator of The *Traditional Witch's Deck*, and he authors a blog on the Patheos Pagan channel called *By Athame and Stang*. In his free time, Kelden enjoys reading, hiking, growing poisonous plants, and playing the ukulele.

Made in United States
Troutdale, OR
07/26/2023

11564647R00051